World Famous
MURIEL
and the Scary Dragon

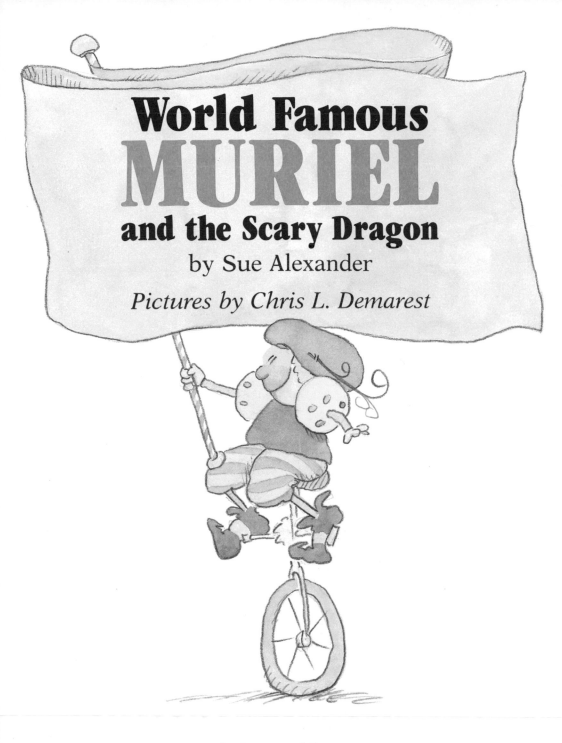

World Famous
MURIEL
and the Scary Dragon
by Sue Alexander

Pictures by Chris L. Demarest

Little, Brown and Company
BOSTON   TORONTO

Library of Congress Cataloging in Publication Data

Alexander, Sue, 1933—
    World famous Muriel and the scary dragon.

    Summary: Muriel is asked by the King to rid the
kingdom of a terrible dragon.
    1. Children's stories, American.   [1. Dragons—
Fiction]   I. Demarest, Chris L., ill.   II. Title.
PZ7.A3784WR   1985   [E]   85-6806
ISBN 0-316-03134-8

AHS

*Published simultaneously in Canada
by Little, Brown & Company (Canada) Limited*

PRINTED IN THE UNITED STATES OF AMERICA

Grolier Enterprises Inc. offers a varied selection of
children's book racks and tote bags. For details on
ordering, please write: Grolier Enterprises Inc.,
Sherman Turnpike, Danbury, CT 06816 Attn:
Premium Department

For Betsy Isele and Chris Demarest,
with love and laughter

— *S.A.*

For Miles and Farley

— *C.L.D.*

6

One day Muriel got a letter.
It said:

Dear Muriel,
You are the best tightrope walker in
the world. You are World Famous. You
are also very smart. You are World
Famous for that, too. I need your help.
Please come right away.
                    Signed,
                    The King of Pompandcircumstance

Muriel thought.
"I will go," she said.

She took her tightrope.
She took peanut butter cookies.
And off she went.

The King was in the dining room.
He was frowning at the food on his
plate.

"What's the matter?" asked Muriel.
"There is a fire-breathing dragon in
the neighborhood," said the King.

"He is scaring everyone. The royal
treasurer is so scared he can't
remember how to count. The jester is
so scared he can't remember how to
jest. And the chef is so scared he
can't remember any of his recipes."
The King burped.

"Not even his recipe for peanut
butter cookies?" asked Muriel.
"No," said the King.

"That's *terrible!*" said Muriel.
"So is this dinner," said the King.
And he burped again.

"Hmmm," said Muriel. "You *do* need
my help."
And she went to the door.

"Where are you going, Muriel?"
asked the King.

14

"I am going to find the dragon,"
Muriel said. "And on the way I will
think very hard. I will think of how
to make him stop scaring everyone."

"Hooray!" said the King.

"It's a good thing I took some peanut
butter cookies with me," Muriel said.
"I do my best thinking when I am
eating them."
She took one out of her bag and
ate it.

Then Muriel went out of the palace.
So did the King.

But they didn't see the dragon
anywhere.

"Hmmm," said Muriel.
And she ate another cookie.

Soon they came to a mountain.
Muriel started up the path.
Then she stopped.

"I have thought of where to find the
dragon," she said.
"Where?" asked the King.
"Somewhere up this mountain,"
Muriel said. "He went this way not
too long ago."

"How do you know, Muriel?" asked
the King.
"The path is still hot," Muriel said.
"My foot is steaming."

"Oh my, so it is," said the King.

Muriel followed the hot path.
The King followed Muriel.
Some clouds were floating around
the mountain.

Muriel walked into one.
So did the King.

"Muriel! I can't see you!" cried the
King. "I can't see *anything*. This
cloud is very dark."
"That's because this cloud is not a
cloud," said Muriel.

"It's not?" said the King.

"No," said Muriel. "It's not. It's smoke."

She ate two more cookies.

"I have thought of something," said
Muriel. "Where there is smoke there
is usually fire."

"That's true," said the King.
"And the dragon breathes fire,"
Muriel went on, "so he is probably
very close."

The King jumped.
"Oh dear!" he said.

Muriel and the King went further up
the mountain.

"Whew!" said the King. "Something
smells *terrible*!"
Muriel wrinkled her nose.
"So it does," she said.

The clouds of smoke got darker.
The terrible smell got stronger.

Suddenly a forked tongue of flame
shot up in front of them.
And a loud ROAR! echoed around
them.
"Help!" wailed the King. "What was
that?"

Muriel peered down into the valley.
"It's just the dragon," she said.
The King ran behind a tree.

Muriel looked at the dark clouds of
smoke. She sniffed the air. She ate
another cookie.
Then she said, "I have thought of
how to make the dragon stop scaring
everyone."
"Oh good!" said the King.

"I will need some soapy water and a
big scrub brush," Muriel said.
"I'll go get them," said the King.
And he did.

Muriel went down her tightrope into
the valley.
"What are you going to do, Muriel?"
called the King.

"Watch!" Muriel called back.

"Ahhhh," breathed the dragon.
He shook himself all over.

38

"My," said the King, "he *does* smell better."
The dragon opened his mouth and puffed out soft clouds of steam.
Muriel ate a cookie.
Then she said, "He won't scare anyone anymore."
"That's a relief!" said the King.
And he came out from behind the tree.

"Muriel," asked the King, "how did you know it was a bath the dragon needed?"

"I thought very hard," Muriel said.

"I thought that if the dragon was
scaring everyone, it was because he
felt angry. How you feel is how you
act."

"That's true," said the King.

"Then I thought," Muriel said, "the dragon was hot. His smoke was very dark. He smelled terrible. He was probably very dirty. And being dirty could make anyone feel angry."

"That is good thinking, Muriel," said
the King. "You are *very* smart!"
"I know," Muriel said.
And she ate some more cookies.

The dragon puffed out more soft
clouds of steam.

"Hmmm," said the King. "The dragon's steam is nice and warm. And my palace is very cold. I think I will take him back to the palace with me. He can be the Royal Steam Heater."

"That's a good idea," Muriel said.
"Then you can give him a bath every
Saturday night."

"So I can," said the King.
And so he did.

Everything was fine in
Pompandcircumstance after that.
The dragon kept the palace nice and
warm.
The royal treasurer remembered how
to count.
The jester remembered how to jest.
The chef remembered all his recipes.

And the King sent World Famous
Muriel a dragon's weight of peanut
butter cookies.